Remarkable Writers

Jeff Kinney

Christine Webster

www.av2books.com

AV² provides enriched content that supplements and complements this book. Weigl's AV² books strive to create inspired learning and engage young minds in a total learning experience.

Your AV² Media Enhanced books come alive with...

Audio
Listen to sections of the book read aloud.

Key Words
Study vocabulary, and complete a matching word activity.

Video
Watch informative video clips.

Quizzes
Test your knowledge.

Embedded Weblinks
Gain additional information for research.

Slide Show
View images and captions, and prepare a presentation.

Try This!
Complete activities and hands-on experiments.

Go to www.av2books.com, and enter this book's unique code.

BOOK CODE

X909286

AV² by Weigl brings you media enhanced books that support active learning.

... and much, much more!

Published by AV² by Weigl
350 5th Avenue, 59th Floor
New York, NY 10118

Website: www.av2books.com   www.weigl.com

Copyright ©2013 AV² by Weigl

Library of Congress Cataloging-in-Publication Data

Webster, Christine.
 Jeff Kinney / Christine Webster and Karen Durrie.
     p. cm. -- (Remarkable writers)
 Includes index.
 ISBN 978-1-61913-058-6 (hard cover : alk. paper) -- ISBN 978-1-61913-598-7 (soft cover : alk. paper) -- ISBN 978-1-61913-721-9 (ebook)
 1. Kinney, Jeff--Juvenile literature. 2. Authors, American--21st century--Biography--Juvenile literature. 3. Children's stories--Authorship--Juvenile literature. I. Durrie, Karen. II. Title.
 PS3611.I634Z93 2013
 813'.6--dc23
 [B]
                              2012003160

Printed in the United States of America in North Mankato, Minnesota
1 2 3 4 5 6 7 8 9 0 16 15 14 13 12

062012
WEP170512

Senior Editor: Heather Kissock
Designer: Terry Paulhus

Weigl acknowledges Getty Images as its primary photo supplier for this title.
Amulet Books (Chad Beckerman/Jeff Kinney): pages 5, 13, 18, 19, 20, 21, 29; Dell Books for Young Readers: page 11.

Contents

AV² Book Code 2

Introducing Jeff Kinney 4

Early Life... 6

Growing Up.. 8

Developing Skills.. 10

Timeline of Jeff Kinney 12

Early Achievements 14

Tricks of the Trade 16

Remarkable Books 18

From Big Ideas to Books 22

Jeff Kinney Today 24

Fan Information 26

Write a Biography 28

Test Yourself.. 29

Writing Terms 30

Key Words/Index 31

Log on to www.av2books.com 32

Introducing Jeff Kinney

Life does not always happen as planned. Sometimes, the road to success is paved with challenges along the way. This is exactly what Jeff Kinney experienced on his way to becoming a best-selling children's author.

Jeff is the author of the popular book series, *Diary of a Wimpy Kid*. The series is about a self-centered seventh grader named Greg Heffley and his life as a middle-school student. The books are filled with jokes, cartoons, and diary-like entries. The books look handwritten and are done in the **first-person** voice of Greg Heffley. The books read like the personal diary of a real boy.

Jeff Kinney's cartoons play a major role in his books.

Jeff's books are in print around the world. More than 50 million copies of the *Wimpy Kid* series have been sold. The books have been **translated** into 35 languages. The first two books in the series have also been turned into hit movies that have made millions of dollars.

Given the popularity of the *Wimpy Kid* series, it is difficult to believe that it took so long for Jeff to find success. The author's unique idea to combine cartoons with text in a book and his perseverance to get his idea **published** eventually paid off.

Jeff Kinney often attends book fairs to sign books for fans.

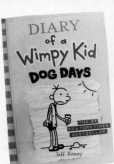
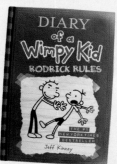
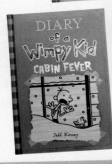

Writing A
Biography

Writers are often inspired to record the stories of people who lead interesting lives. The story of another person's life is known as a biography. A biography can tell the story of any person, from authors such as Jeff Kinney, to inventors, presidents, and sports stars.

When writing a biography, authors must first collect information about their subject. This information may come from a book about the person's life, a news article about one of his or her accomplishments, or a review of his or her work. Libraries and the internet will have much of this information. Most biographers will also interview their subjects. Personal accounts provide a great deal of information and a unique point of view. When some basic details about the person's life have been collected, it is time to begin writing a biography.

As you read about Jeff Kinney, you will be introduced to the important parts of a biography. Use these tips, and the examples provided, to learn how to write about an author or any other remarkable person.

Early Life

Jeff Kinney spent his childhood in Fort Washington, Maryland, near Washington, D.C. He grew up with two brothers and a sister. His sister was the eldest child, and Jeff was the middle boy between older and younger brothers.

"I was kind of an ordinary child... I was kind of quiet, fairly smart, not very outspoken."
—*Jeff Kinney*

Jeff's father worked in the navy. He loved to read the newspaper each day. His father also collected **comics** dated from the 1940s and 1950s. Jeff loved to read the comic books. He learned to appreciate comic strips and books for their unique way of combining jokes, artwork, and storytelling. Comics had a huge **influence** on Jeff later becoming a **cartoonist** and writer.

Donald Duck and Scrooge McDuck were two of Jeff's favorite cartoon characters when he was young.

His mother was also very influential in his life. She was a teacher who raised her family while going to college to get her **doctorate.** Jeff greatly admired her determination.

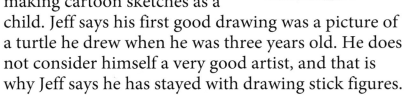

Jeff began doodling when he was very young. He was always making cartoon sketches as a child. Jeff says his first good drawing was a picture of a turtle he drew when he was three years old. He does not consider himself a very good artist, and that is why Jeff says he has stayed with drawing stick figures.

Like many siblings, Jeff and his brothers did not always get along. The characters in Jeff's books, Greg Heffley and his bullyish older brother, Rodrick, share similar experiences to Jeff's real-life childhood. Like the character of Rodrick, Jeff's older brother Scott was in a band that rehearsed in the basement. However, Jeff says Scott is really much nicer than Rodrick.

The community of Fort Washington was named for a nearby fort. Built in 1809, it protected the city of Washington, D.C.

Writing About Early Life

A person's early years have a strong influence on his or her future. Parents, teachers, and friends can have a large impact on how a person thinks, feels, and behaves. These effects are strong enough to last throughout childhood, and often a person's lifetime.

In order to write about a person's early life, biographers must find answers to the following questions.

1 Where and when was the person born?

2 What is known about the person's family and friends?

3 Did the person grow up in unusual circumstances?

Growing Up

Jeff was an average kid growing up. He was on the school swim team, but he did not always make it to practices. Instead of going to practice, he would sometimes go to the creek. He would collect tadpoles and play in the water. Missing swim practice stopped when his parents arrived early to pick him up and saw him walk into the pool area holding a bag of tadpoles.

"'I feel blessed to have had a really ordinary childhood, because the stories I write are all very ordinary."
—*Jeff Kinney*

His swim team experiences inspired more than one **passage** in the *Wimpy Kid* books. For example, Greg hides from his swim coach in *Rodrick Rules* by ducking into the locker room and wrapping himself in toilet paper to keep warm. Jeff actually did this when he was a boy. Jeff remembered this and other episodes from his childhood and used them to help him create his stories.

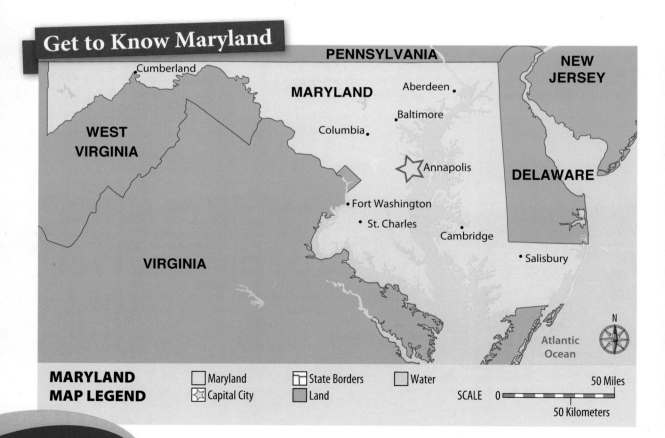

Get to Know Maryland

PENNSYLVANIA
Cumberland
MARYLAND
Aberdeen
NEW JERSEY
Baltimore
Columbia
WEST VIRGINIA
Annapolis
DELAWARE
Fort Washington
St. Charles
Cambridge
VIRGINIA
Salisbury
Atlantic Ocean
N

MARYLAND MAP LEGEND
Maryland
Capital City
State Borders
Land
Water
SCALE 0
50 Miles
50 Kilometers

As a student, Jeff was also average. He found chemistry the most difficult subject in school, and he struggled to pass the class. He liked English best because he enjoyed writing stories.

Jeff liked to read and was inspired by many different authors. He read books by Judy Blume, Beverly Cleary, Piers Anthony, and J.R.R. Tolkien. His favorite comics included *Calvin and Hobbes* by Bill Watterson, *Bloom County* by Berkeley Breathed, and *The Far Side* by Gary Larson. Reading those comics, Jeff felt the first stirrings of wanting to be a cartoonist himself.

Jeff also began dabbling in computer programming after his mother bought an Apple computer for the family. Computer programming would later become Jeff's career.

🐚 An Apple computer is better known as MacIntosh or Mac. Apple is the name of the company that develops these computers.

Writing About
Growing Up

Some people know what they want to achieve in life from a very young age. Others do not decide until much later. In any case, it is important for biographers to discuss when and how their subjects make these decisions. Using the information they collect, biographers try to answer the following questions about their subjects' paths in life.

1 Who had the most influence on the person?

2 Did he or she receive assistance from others?

3 Did the person have a positive attitude?

Developing Skills

Many of Jeff's story ideas come from his childhood. Writers are often keen observers and pay close attention to what is happening around them. Jeff kept a vivid memory of his childhood. His adventures on the swim team, playing soccer, and going to school all became part of his books.

"I think that stories with characters who always do the right thing are a little boring."
—*Jeff Kinney*

Several of the people in his books came from childhood memories of family life. For instance, the author claims that he modeled Greg Heffley after his own worst traits. Jeff also took all the mean things that he and his brothers did as children, and used them to create Greg's older bother Roderick.

Most ideas for the *Wimpy Kid* series come from everyday life. Kinney still remembers what it was like to be in the seventh grade.

Jeff had to rely on his memory for these story ideas because he did not keep a journal when he was a boy. He only began keeping a journal of his own when he was older. He did this because he felt he was wasting time watching television and playing video games. He created a journal to document what he did every day. He wanted to be sure that he was using his time effectively.

Writing in a journal was also a way for Jeff to encourage his drawing. He wanted to make sure that he remained focused on developing his cartooning skills. The journal became a place where he could draw and scribble jokes. Before long, he had built up hundreds of jokes. After reviewing them, he began to sort through them to find the best ones. He then began trying to create a story **plot** from the jokes.

Writing About Developing Skills

Every remarkable person has skills and traits that make him or her noteworthy. Some people have natural talent, while others practice diligently. For most, it is a combination of the two. One of the most important things that a biographer can do is to tell the story of how their subject developed his or her talents.

1 What was the person's education?

2 What was the person's first job or work experience?

3 What obstacles did the person overcome?

Jeff's favorite book growing up was Judy Blume's *Tales of a Fourth Grade Nothing.* Blume is also a best-selling author, and, like Jeff, she has a unique ability to write from a child's perspective.

Timeline of Jeff Kinney

1971

Jeff Kinney is born in Maryland on February 19. He is the third of four children.

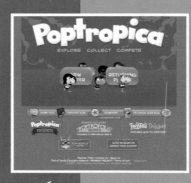

2007

Jeff designs the websi Poptropica.com, a fun gaming website for children.

2006

Jeff presents the *Wimpy Kid* idea to an **editor** at the first New York City Comic Con.

NEW YORK COMIC CON

1993

Jeff graduates from the University of Maryland with a degree in **criminology**. While at university, Jeff becomes well known for his comic *Igdoof*, which runs in the college paper, *The Diamondback*.

1998

Jeff begins writing journal entries and sketches for *Diary of a Wimpy Kid*.

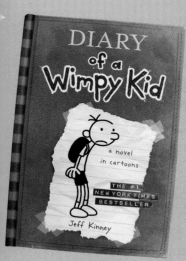

2011

Diary of a Wimpy Kid: Cabin Fever, the sixth book in the series, is published. Six million copies are printed for the book's release.

2011

A second *Wimpy Kid* movie, *Diary of a Wimpy Kid: Rodrick Rules*, is released. It makes more than $23 million on its opening weekend.

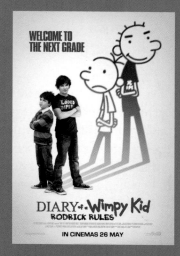

2007

The first *Diary of a Wimpy Kid* is published, and 13,000 copies are printed. It quickly becomes a bestseller. To date, it has spent more than 158 weeks on the New York Times Best Seller list.

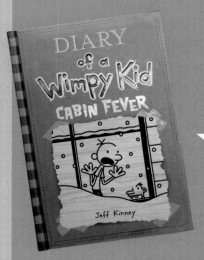

TIME

2010

The *Diary of a Wimpy Kid* movie is released in theaters. It **grosses** more than $76 million around the world.

2009

Jeff is named one of the 100 most influential people by *Time* magazine. The list also includes Barack Obama and Oprah Winfrey.

Early Achievements

In the early 1990s, Jeff was a young man making his way through college. After a year of studying computer programming at Villanova University, he became a criminology student at the University of Maryland. In his first year of university, he created a comic strip called *Igdoof*. It was **rejected** several times before it was finally published in the campus newspaper. With the move to a new college, *Igdoof* found a home in the pages of the University of Maryland's campus paper, *The Diamondback*. This was a very exciting time for Jeff. He was writing a cartoon read by thousands of people each day. The experience made him want to become a professional newspaper cartoonist. He began to get attention from the **media** for the comic strip.

"I've always wanted to be a cartoonist, and I've always had an interest in computer programming. So in a sense, I got to be exactly what I hoped to be when I was younger."
—*Jeff Kinney*

Jeff was interviewed by the *Washington Post* and the *Baltimore Sun* about the success of *Igdoof*. After the success of *Igdoof*, Jeff thought it would be easy to get published in larger city newspapers.

Comcast Center is one of the University of Maryland's newer buildings. Completed in 2002, it houses offices, study areas, a gymnasium, and a banquet hall.

After college, Jeff kept trying to get his work published in city newspapers, but received rejection after rejection. For three years, he tried to get his cartoon **syndicated** in a newspaper, but he was not successful. He felt very discouraged. Not only was the **market** for syndication shrinking, Jeff began to believe that his work might not be as good as he thought. Jeff soon began to think that he might not become a newspaper cartoonist.

Still, this did not keep him from drawing. Jeff began keeping a diary filled with cartoons. This inspired a new idea. Jeff decided to write a fictional story in a cartoon-style format, from the point of view of a seventh grade boy. The idea for *Diary of a Wimpy Kid* was born. While Jeff began to work on this new idea, he also became a website developer. He worked on a website called Funbrain.com and began to upload his *Wimpy Kid* cartoons to it. The cartoons became an online hit. Jeff also created the website Poptropica.com in 2007. Four years later, this site was named one of the 50 best websites by *Time* magazine.

Writing About

Early Achievements

No two people take the same path to success. Some people work very hard for a long time before achieving their goals. Others may take advantage of a fortunate turn of events. Biographers must make special note of the traits and qualities that allow their subjects to succeed.

1 What was the person's most important early success?

2 What process does the person use in his or her work?

3 Which of the person's traits were most helpful in his or her work?

The Funbrain website hosts educational games and activities for kids of all ages.

Tricks of the Trade

Writing a story or a poem can be challenging, but it can also be very rewarding. Some writers have trouble finding ideas, while others have so many ideas that they do not know where to start. Jeff Kinney has special writing habits that young writers can follow to develop their ideas into great stories.

Keep Your Eyes and Ears Open

Many writers get ideas by watching people and listening to conversations. If you pay attention, you will see that most people say and do all sorts of interesting things. Observing people can inspire writers to develop characters or to write funny scenes. To create his stories, Jeff Kinney spends time looking back to his childhood in school and at home to recall what people said and did.

Write, Write, Write

Sometimes, the easiest way to finish a poem or a story is to write as much as possible in a first **draft**. This way, a writer can get all of his or her ideas down on paper. Then, the writer can decide which parts to keep. Very few writers have ever produced a great story in just one draft. Instead, they may review their first draft to see which parts should stay and what needs to be **revised**. Each of Jeff's books contains about 350 jokes. It can take him hours just to write one joke, and about nine months of hard work to write and illustrate a book. In that time, Jeff writes hundreds of jokes and story ideas. Only his best ideas make it into his books.

The Creative Process

Most writers have different opinions about the best time to write. Some work best late at night when everyone else is asleep. Others are most productive early in the morning. There are also differing approaches to the writing process. Some writers need to make a detailed outline. This is a good idea for new writers as it helps them organize their thoughts. Some writers do not use an outline. They simply begin writing and let their ideas flow. Jeff's approach to writing is unusual. He lays on his couch with a blanket over his head and writes out his ideas.

"The whole process is terribly time consuming, and not that fun, but my greatest joy in life is to come up with a joke — an original joke. And so, it's fun in the end."
—*Jeff Kinney*

It Takes Dedication

Jeff works during the day as a web designer. Often, when he is writing a new book, he does so at night after spending a couple of hours with his family. He writes and draws from 8 p.m. until 4 a.m., sleeps for a couple of hours, and then goes to work. He may work this way for two months until a book is finished.

Jeff likes to spend time with his fans. By getting to know them, he can develop stories about subjects that matter to them.

Remarkable Books

Each *Diary of a Wimpy Kid* book is 224 pages long and printed in handwritten style, with cartoon drawings sprinkled throughout. There are six books in the series, and Jeff hopes to write 10 in total. Jeff has decided that Greg Heffley will remain the same age throughout the books, the same way many of his favorite comic book characters did.

Diary of a Wimpy Kid

It is a new school year, and Greg Heffley is in the seventh grade. He spends his school days with a mix of wimpy kids and kids that are bigger, meaner, and more mature. His mother makes him keep a diary, which Greg insists is a "journal." Greg has his best friend, Rowley, to help him get through the trials of each day. When Rowley starts to become popular, Greg tries to take advantage of Rowley's new status. When Greg lets Rowley take the blame for something, it has tough consequences on their friendship.

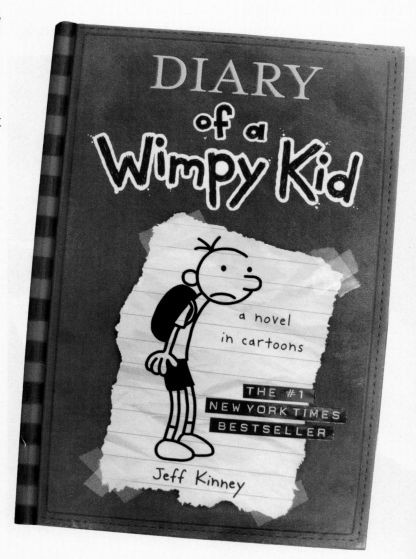

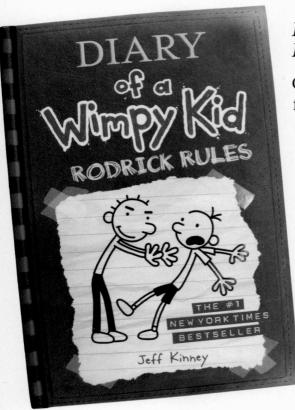

Diary of a Wimpy Kid: Rodrick Rules

Greg Heffley has had a rotten summer. His father makes him join the swim team. Greg is miserable about this. To make matters worse, his older brother, Rodrick, now knows all of Greg's embarrassing secrets because he read Greg's diary. Greg's little brother Manny is driving him crazy. After summer vacation, Greg returns to school and has to deal with the stresses of middle school, his secret getting out, trying to impress girls, and avoiding the school talent show.

Diary of a Wimpy Kid: The Last Straw

The second half of Greg's seventh grade year is documented in this book. The new year starts off with the Heffley family deciding to work on self-improvement. Greg already thinks he is the best person he knows. Greg's father is getting tired of Greg's wimpy ways and threatens to enroll his son in military school during summer vacation. Greg tries to change his dad's mind, offering to play soccer and join boy scouts instead.

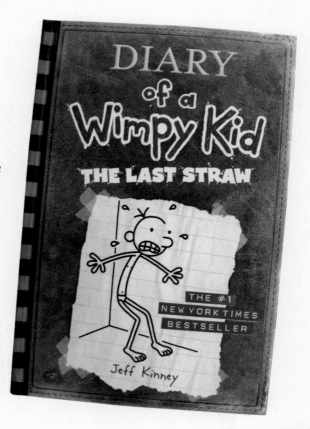

Diary of a Wimpy Kid: Dog Days

The fourth book in the series documents Greg Heffley's summer vacation. Everyone is having fun outside, but Greg is happily sitting indoors. Most days, he keeps the shades down and plays video games. He is living his ultimate dream of having no responsibilities or rules. However, his fantasy summer does not last long. Greg's mom decides the family needs to spend more time together. To Greg's horror, his mother creates a book club for boys. To ruin his summer further, Greg and his best friend Rowley start a lawn-care business later in the summer to pay off a debt. The business fails, and the friends have an argument.

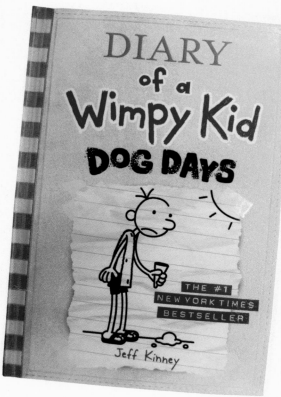

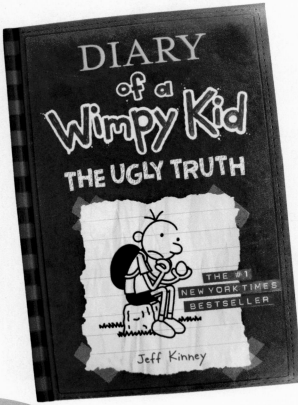

Diary of a Wimpy Kid: The Ugly Truth

In this book, Greg Heffley faces the pressure of boy-girl parties and new responsibilities. This diary also deals with the funny and awkward changes pre-teens go through as they grow up. Greg deals with all these changes without his best friend Rowley because they are no longer friends. Growing up, Greg decides, is overrated.

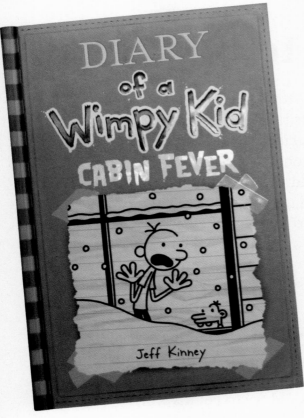

Diary of a Wimpy Kid: Cabin Fever

In this book, Greg Heffley is facing a world of trouble. Greg is the prime suspect after school property is vandalized. As school authorities close in on him, a sudden blizzard hits the town. The Heffley family is cooped up inside their house. Greg wonders if there could be any worse punishment than being trapped indoors with his family over the winter break. To make matters worse, Greg also must stay on his best behavior under the threat of no presents from Santa.

Diary of a Wimpy Kid: Do-It-Yourself Book

Aspiring writers inspired by the *Wimpy Kid* series can create their own similar diary using the *Do-It-Yourself Book*. The book offers humorous writing prompts, questions, lists, and comics that help readers tell their own life stories. The second half of the book contains room for readers to draw their own cartoons and to keep a daily journal. The end result is a diary that looks much like *Wimpy Kid* Greg Heffley's diary.

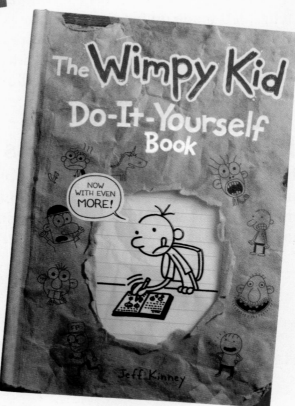

From Big Ideas to Books

Jeff began writing *Diary of a Wimpy Kid* very quickly. After a while, he realized that much of what he was writing was not very funny. This was very disappointing to him. He decided he needed another plan. Before he started writing an actual book, he dedicated his time to coming up with 77 idea pages. He would sketch and write all of his ideas on these pages. From here, he would choose only the very best ideas for the book. It took Jeff four years to fill those 77 idea pages. He then cut 80 percent of the material he felt was not worth putting in the book. Even after cutting that much, Jeff was still left with enough ideas to make a book.

"It took about eleven years to write the first three books, but now, I have to turn each one out in about nine months."
—*Jeff Kinney*

After his newspaper cartoon rejections, Jeff decided that he needed to refocus his writing. With his collection of journal entries and sketches, Jeff made up his mind that he would try to get his work published in book form. He was not sure his diary idea would ever have a chance of being published. The idea might be too unusual for the market, as it was handwritten and illustrated with cartoons.

The Publishing Process

Publishing companies receive hundreds of **manuscripts** from authors each year. Only a few manuscripts become books. Publishers must be sure that a manuscript will sell many copies. As a result, publishers reject most of the manuscripts they receive. Once a manuscript has been accepted, it goes through

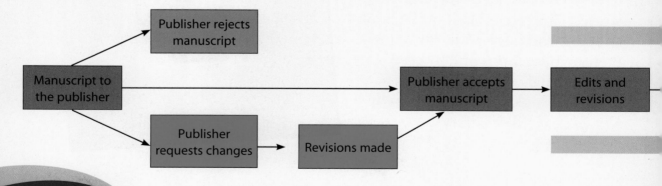

Jeff was determined to get published, even if he had to find an unusual way of getting his book noticed. In 2006, Jeff took a sample pack of his cartoons for the *Diary of a Wimpy Kid* idea to the New York Comic-Con, which is a **popular culture** convention. Here, he met Charlie Kochman, a comic book editor. Jeff pitched his idea for the book, which he intended to be read by adults, to Charlie. Charlie immediately liked it. He took Jeff's material to his publishing team. Here, the idea of making *Wimpy Kid* a series for kids was brought up. Jeff was skeptical it would work as a children's book, but agreed to revise *Wimpy Kid* for younger readers. Charlie later became Jeff Kinney's editor.

At Comic Con, fans can come face-to-face with some of their favorite comic book, video, and movie characters.

many stages before it is published. Often, authors change their work to follow an editor's suggestions. Once the book is published, some authors receive royalties. This is money based on book sales.

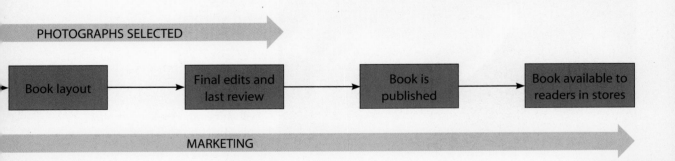

PHOTOGRAPHS SELECTED

Book layout → Final edits and last review → Book is published → Book available to readers in stores

MARKETING

Jeff Kinney Today

Jeff Kinney is grateful for his success. Even with the money *Wimpy Kid* has made for him, he continues to live a regular life. He has the same job he had before *Wimpy Kid* became a bestseller. He drives the same car. He plays ball with his kids and rides his bike around the neighborhood.

Jeff lives in Plainville, Massachusetts. He enjoys that he is not often recognized or treated like a celebrity. He has helped out family members and given charitable donations. He also intends to provide funding to make improvements to facilities in Plainville.

Jeff's books and movies have made him a wealthy man. His one splurge has been to purchase the house next to his own. Jeff uses the small house as an office where he can write away from his home. Before buying his writing house, he would write in hotel rooms because he needed the space and silence.

🖐 Jeff loves to spend time with his wife, Julie, and their two boys, Will and Grant. He likes to play volleyball and watch television.

Even after publishing many successful books, Jeff still finds writing and drawing a challenge. He thinks of himself as an illustrator first and a writer second. Illustrating can be a challenge when his books require at least 1,000 **illustrations** each. Sometimes, the joy of illustrating can be affected by the amount of time it actually takes. When all is said and done, Jeff says he still loves the process of seeing his words and cartoons come together. Jeff is also extremely proud that his *Wimpy Kid* series has been credited with getting more children to read books and to think that reading is cool.

Writing About the Person Today

The biography of any living person is an ongoing story. People have new ideas, start new projects, and deal with challenges. For their work to be meaningful, biographers must include up-to-date information about their subjects. Through research, biographers try to answer the following questions.

1 Has the person received awards or recognition for accomplishments?

2 What is the person's life's work?

3 How have the person's accomplishments served others?

In 2011, an enormous *Wimpy Kid* balloon floated down the streets of New York City in the annual Macy's Thanksgiving Day Parade. Jeff was thrilled to have one of his characters in this parade alongside other well-known cartoons.

Fan Information

F ans of Jeff Kinney will be able to enjoy *Wimpy Kid* for some time to come. The books continue to be bestsellers, and Jeff has said he will write more in the series before turning his attention to a new project. Fans can read *Wimpy Kid* comics online at Funbrain.com. Jeff's daytime work as a web designer can also be seen and played in the games on Poptropica.com. The site includes an area called *Wimpy Wonderland*, a virtual world based on Jeff's books.

Jeff attended the premiere of *Diary of a Wimpy Kid* with Robert Capron and Zachary Gordon. Zachary played wimpy kid Greg Heffley in the movie, and Robert played best friend Rowley Jefferson.

Fans can also enjoy *Wimpy Kid* on video and at the movie theater. Kinney was excited to be part of the movie-making process. He assisted screenwriters with the script, helped to cast the characters, and was on set while the movies were being made. Kinney says that choosing the actor to play Greg Heffley was a challenge. In the book, Greg's defining characteristics are three hairs on his head and bad posture. Those in charge of casting the film looked for a thin boy who was flawed, but also likable. Kinney was also involved in doing the animation for the parts of the movies that bring Greg's cartoon diary drawings to life.

Wimpy Kid cartoons can be read online on the official *Diary of a Wimpy Kid* website at www.wimpykid.com. Here, fans can find out more about Kinney and his books, read news, and access video and audio clips. The site includes a list of Kinney's favorite website links and a schedule of appearances he plans to make to promote his books.

The Diary of a Wimpy Kid website provides all the latest news on Jeff and his books.

Write a Biography

All of the parts of a biography work together to tell the story of a person's life. Find out how these elements combine by writing a biography. Begin by choosing a person whose story fascinates you. You will have to research the person's life by using library books and reliable websites. You can also email the person or write him or her a letter. The person might agree to answer your questions directly.

Use a concept web, such as the one below, to guide you in writing the biography. Answer each of the questions listed using the information you have gathered. Each heading on the concept web will form an important part of the person's story.

Parts of a Biography

Early Life
Where and when was the person born?

What is known about the person's family and friends?

Did the person grow up in unusual circumstances?

Growing Up
Who had the most influence on the person?

Did he or she receive assistance from others?

Did the person have a positive attitude?

Developing Skills
What was the person's education?

What was the person's first job or work experience?

What obstacles did the person overcome?

Person Today
Has the person received awards or recognition for accomplishments?

What is the person's life's work?

How have the person's accomplishments served others?

Early Achievements
What was the person's most important early success?

What processes does this person use in his or her work?

Which of the person's traits were most helpful in his or her work?

Test Yourself

1 What was the name of the comic strip Kinney published in college?

2 Who is Greg Heffley's best friend?

3 Where did the *Wimpy Kid* cartoons first appear online?

4 What year did Kinney first start keeping journals?

5 Which magazine named Kinney one of the 100 most influential people in 2011?

6 What is the name of Greg Heffley's brother?

7 Where does Jeff Kinney live?

8 In what year was the first *Wimpy Kid* book published?

9 What real incident from Kinney's childhood was put in a *Wimpy Kid* book?

10 Name Jeff Kinney's favorite childhood book.

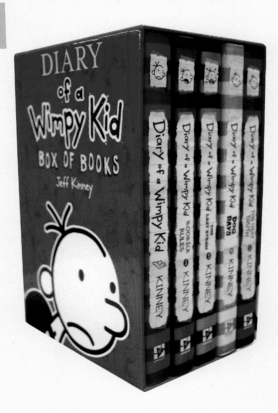

ANSWERS
1. *Igdoof* 2. Rowley 3. On Funbrain.com 4. 1998 5. *Time Magazine* 6. Rodrick 7. Plainville, Massachusetts 8. 2007 9. Kinney hid in a locker room and wrapped himself in toilet paper 10. *Tales of a Fourth Grade Nothing*

Writing Terms

The field of writing has its own language. Understanding some of the more common writing terms will allow you to discuss your ideas about books.

action: the moving events of a work of fiction

antagonist: the person in the story who opposes the main character

autobiography: a history of a person's life written by that person

biography: a written account of another person's life

character: a person in a story, poem, or play

climax: the most exciting moment or turning point in a story

episode: a scene or short piece of action in a story

fiction: stories about characters and events that are not real

foreshadow: hinting at something that is going to happen later in the book

imagery: a written description of a thing or idea that brings an image to mind

narrator: the speaker of the story who relates the events

nonfiction: writing that deals with real people and events

novel: published writing of considerable length that portrays characters within a story

plot: the order of events in a work of fiction

protagonist: the leading character of a story; often a likable character

resolution: the end of the story, when the conflict is settled

scene: a single episode in a story

setting: the place and time in which a work of fiction occurs

theme: an idea that runs throughout a work of fiction

Key Words

cartoonist: a person who draws pictures representing people, subjects, and actions

comics: stories written in short form, often inside blocks or strips, with drawings

criminology: the scientific study of crime and criminals

doctorate: the highest academic degree in a field

draft: a rough copy of a story

editor: someone who manages part of a publishing firm

first-person: when a story is narrated by the main character

grosses: total amount of sales something makes

illustrations: drawings

influence: the ability to have an effect on someone or something

manuscript: a draft of a story before it is published

market: the demand for a specific product

media: means of communication, such as newspaper, radio,television, and magazines

passage: a portion of a written work

plot: the order of events in a work of fiction

popular culture: activites and products, including video games, movies, books, music, video games, toys, and television shows, that are popular with many people

published: to be printed and distributed for sale

rejected: not accepted

revised: changed

syndicated: when work is bought by an agency to be published in many publications at one time

translated: turning from one language into another language

Index

cartoonist 6, 9, 14, 15

Diamondback, The 12, 14
Diary of a Wimpy Kid 4, 12, 13, 15, 18, 22, 23, 27
Diary of a Wimpy Kid: Cabin Fever 13, 21
Diary of a Wimpy Kid: Do-It-Yourself Book 21
Diary of a Wimpy Kid: Dog Days 20
Diary of a Wimpy Kid: Rodrick Rules 8, 13, 19

Diary of a Wimpy Kid: The Last Straw 19
Diary of a Wimpy Kid: The Ugly Truth 20

Fort Washington, Maryland 6, 7
Funbrain.com 15, 26, 29

Igdoof 12, 14, 29

journal 11, 12, 18, 21, 22, 29

Kochman, Charlie 23

movie 5, 13, 23, 24, 26, 27

Plainville, Massachusetts 24, 29
Poptropica.com 12, 15, 26

Time Magazine 13, 15, 29

University of Maryland 12, 14

Log on to www.av2books.com

AV² by Weigl brings you media enhanced books that support active learning. Go to www.av2books.com, and enter the special code found on page 2 of this book. You will gain access to enriched and enhanced content that supplements and complements this book. Content includes video, audio, weblinks, quizzes, a slide show, and activities.

Audio
Listen to sections of the book read aloud.

Video
Watch informative video clips.

Embedded Weblinks
Gain additional information for research.

Try This!
Complete activities and hands-on experiments.

WHAT'S ONLINE?

Try This!	Embedded Weblinks	Video	EXTRA FEATURES
Complete an activity about your childhood.	Learn more about Jeff Kinney's life.	Watch a video about Jeff Kinney.	
Try this timeline activity.	Learn more about Jeff Kinney's achievements.	Watch this interview with Jeff Kinney.	
See what you know about the publishing process.	Check out this site about Jeff Kinney.		
Test your knowledge of writing terms.			
Write a biography.			

Audio
Listen to sections of the book read aloud.

Key Words
Study vocabulary, and complete a matching word activity.

Slide Show
View images and captions, and prepare a presentation.

Quizzes
Test your knowledge.

AV² was built to bridge the gap between print and digital. We encourage you to tell us what you like and what you want to see in the future.
Sign up to be an AV² Ambassador at www.av2books.com/ambassador.